Dear Henrique!
Keep being so
creative and curious. It
is a pleasure working with you!
"The imagination is the golden pathway
to everywhere." ~ Terence McKenna
♡ Miss Colleen

HARVEY
THE
CHILD
MIME

BY LORYN BRANTZ

This book belongs to ___Henrique___ ,the Child Mime.

HOMETOWN 520 LLC

Text and illustrations copyright © 2010 by Loryn Brantz

HOMETOWN 520 LLC

Hometown 520
PO Box 1041
Darien, CT 06820

ISBN-10   0-9822205-8-8
ISBN-13   9780982220580

CPSIA Compliance Information: This book was manufactured by Regal Printing Limited in Hong Kong September 2010, Job #1007082

Printed in Hong Kong

www.HarveyMimes.com

HARVEY THE CHILD MIME

LORYN BRANTZ

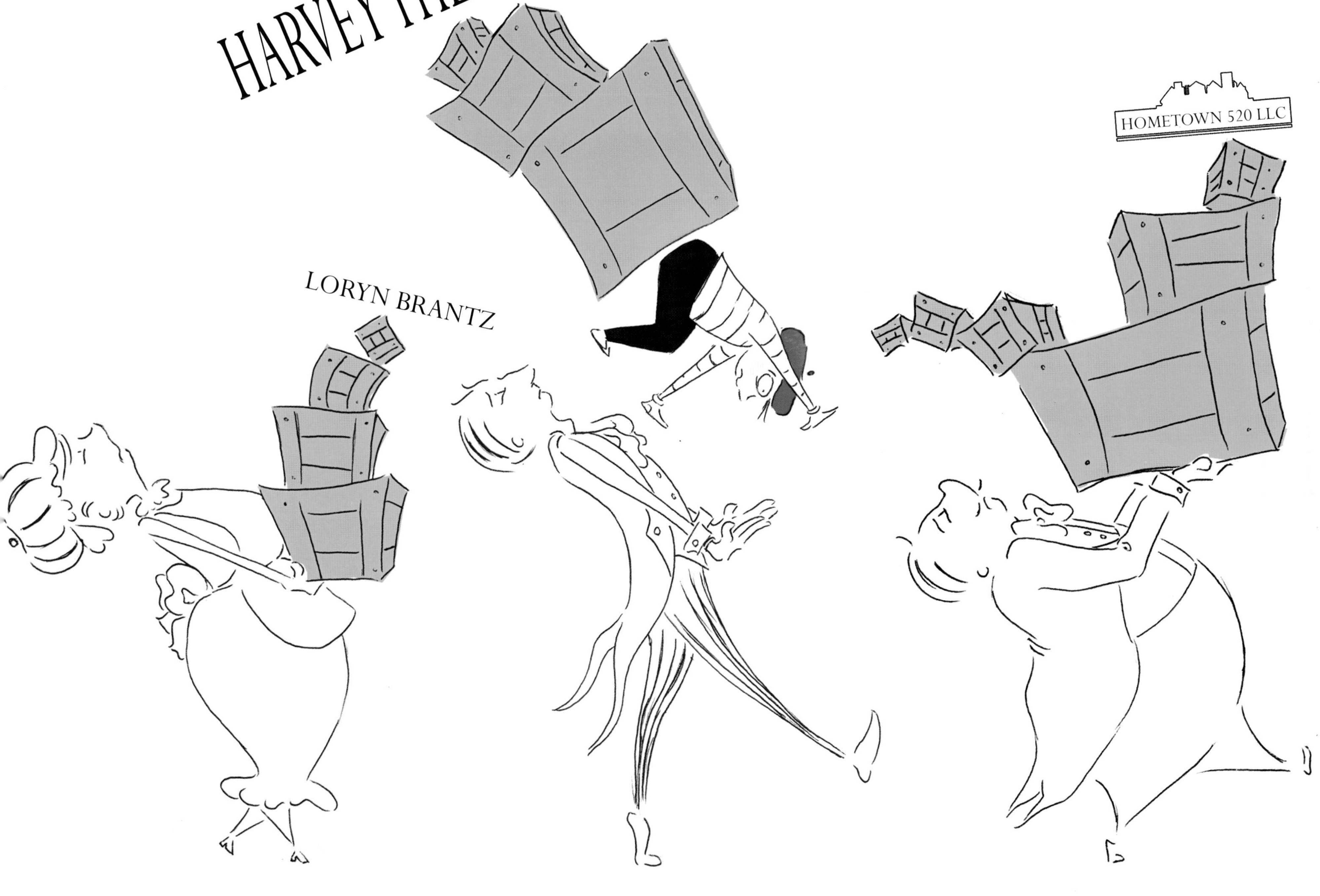

HOMETOWN 520 LLC

Every morning Harvey puts on his most favorite striped shirt . . .

. . . and his most reddest red hat

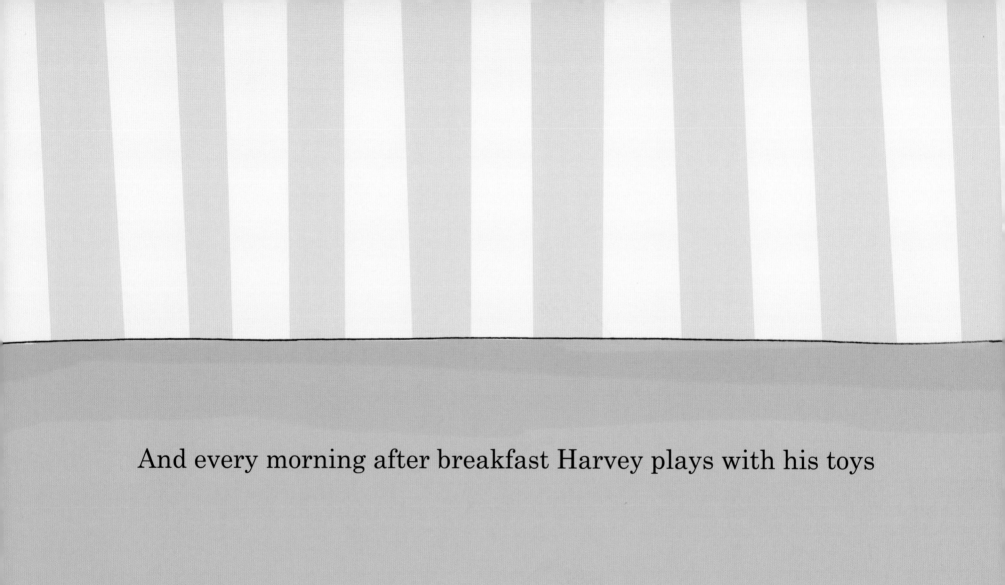

And every morning after breakfast Harvey plays with his toys while his father reads the paper.

His father is a man of few words...
no words, to be exact.

Harvey comes from a family of mimes.

When the sun hits the center of the sky and the clock says noon

Harvey makes his way to the docks to do what he does best.

And every day, Harvey gets up on his apple box
and people crowd around to watch him perform.

He pretends to be pulling a bus full of rhinos with one single rope!

He pretends to be rowing a canoe through a beautiful lagoon.

And every day he pretends to be trapped in *a box*.

On this particular day, during this particular act, he must have been performing the very best invisible box he ever had, because two workers at the dock mistook his box for one of their own and loaded him onto a cargo ship.

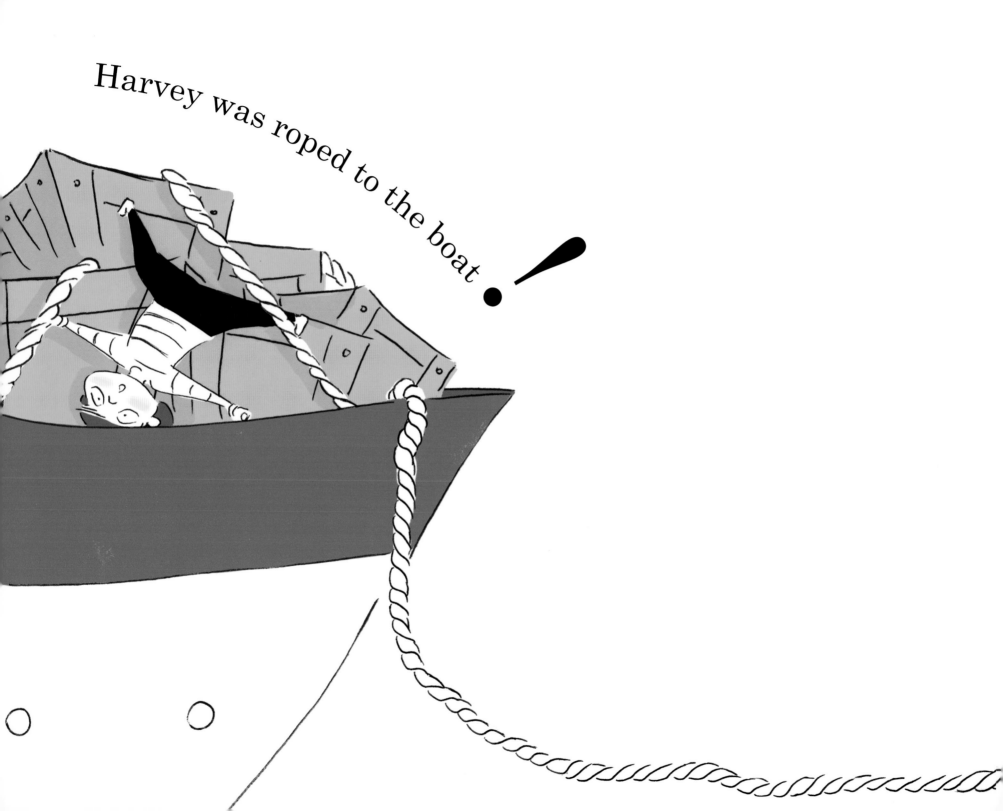

"At least this boat is roped to the dock," Harvey thought to himself.

But it wasn't docked for long.

"I bet this boat won't go very far," Harvey assured himself.

But again, Harvey was wrong. The boat sailed...

and sailed...

and sailed...

and sailed...

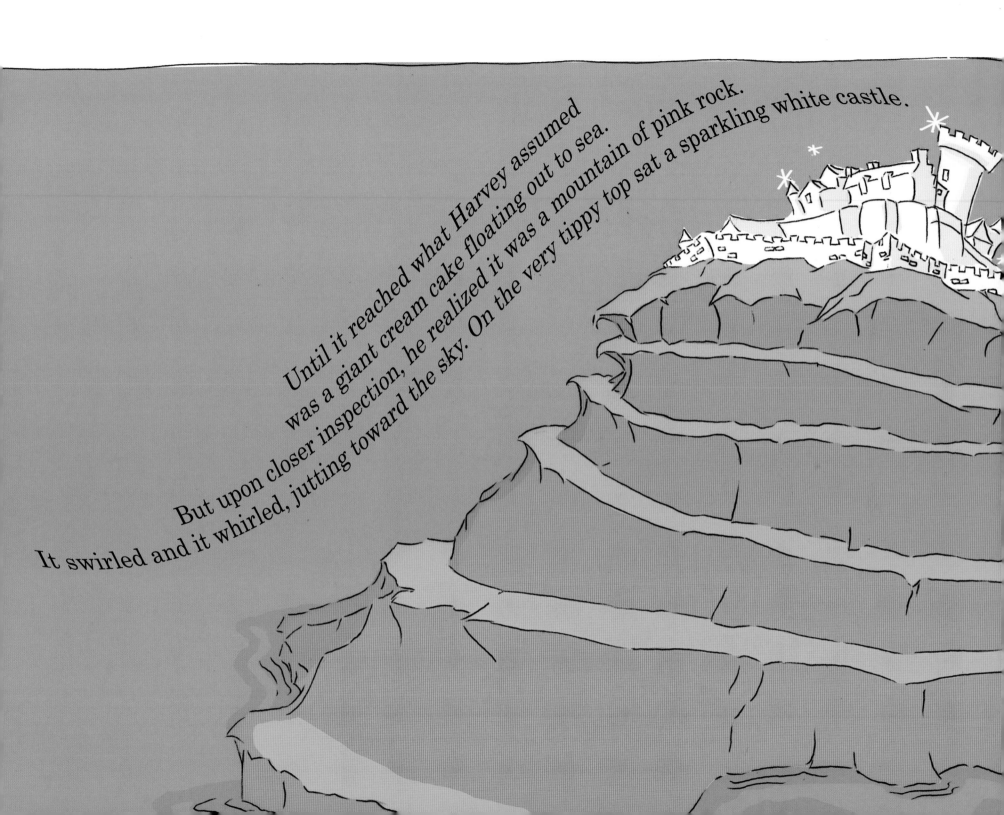

Until it reached what Harvey assumed
was a giant cream cake floating out to sea.
But upon closer inspection, he realized it was a mountain of pink rock.
It swirled and it whirled, jutting toward the sky. On the very tippy top sat a sparkling white castle.

Butlers and maids hustled down the pink pathways.

They
quickly retrieved
all of the
boxes on the boat,
including the box
containing
Harvey.

"I'm certain someone will notice
me in this invisible box,"
Harvey comforted himself.

But once again, Harvey was wrong.
He was swiftly taken to a room
with the other boxes to be wrapped.

The freshly wrapped boxes were piled into a room.
The room belonged to Princess Mindy.
It was her birthday!
Although, it was not that exciting,
for she throws a party for herself
twice a day,
every day.

The maids and butlers shook nervously in the corner hoping
Princess Mindy would be pleased with her presents.
Although, every day, twice a day she is not.

Princess Mindy ravingly ripped the wrapping off the boxes.

Carefully curled ribbons went flying through the air.

"This puppy's nose is **too wet!**" she cried.

"This doll's curls are **too curly!**"

"This jeweled crown does **not** have enough jewels!" she proclaimed.

Frustrated, Princess Mindy grabbed the next box within reach.

"Someone unwrapped me, they are sure to send me home now!" Harvey thought.

"I WANTED A PONY NOT A LITTLE BOY!"

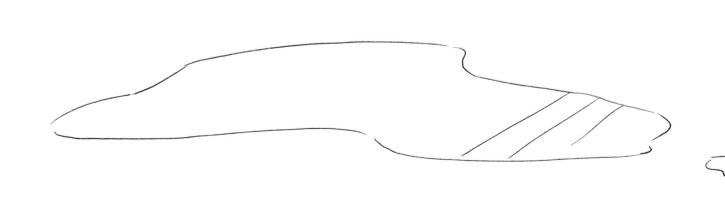

Startled and confused by the Princess's reaction to him, Harvey tried to comfort her. But his attempts were only met with louder screams.

"BWAHHHH!"

Baffled by the Princess's behavior,
Harvey knew to get home he would have to take matters into his own hands.
He imagined a horse and mounted it, preparing to ride it home.

Princess Mindy's cries came to a halt.
She focused her wet eyes on Harvey's invisible horse.

The maids and butlers dashed out of the room to
find an invisible horse for the Princess.

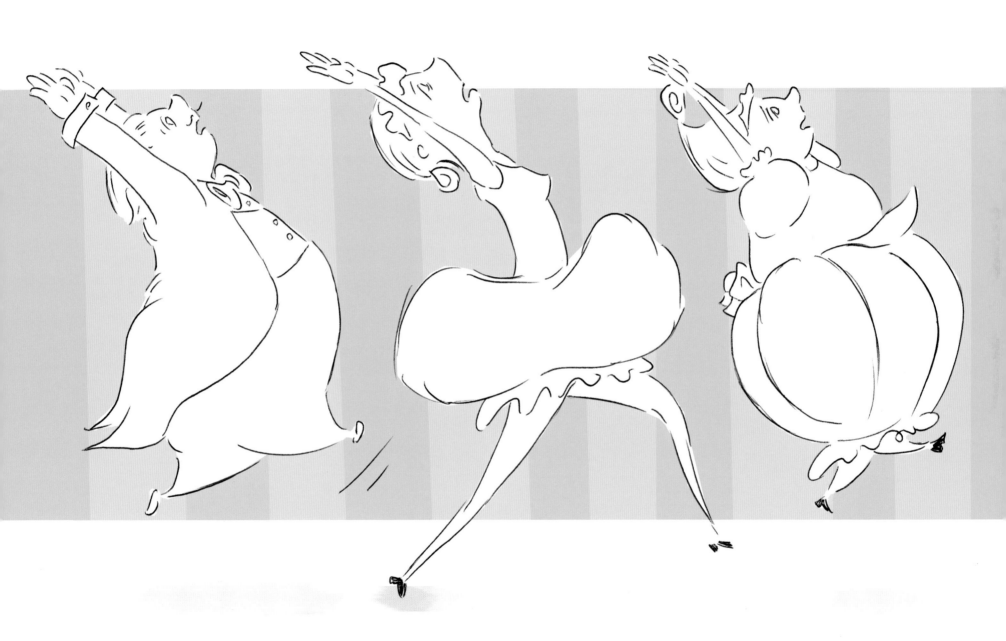

Harvey knew their search would be to no avail,
as one cannot buy an invisible horse.

Feeling sorry for the Princess,
who was now splashing and flopping around in puddles of tears,
Harvey reached down and pulled her up onto the horse.

In that moment, it hit Princess Mindy like a slap of swiss cheese to the face!
To have an invisible horse, she only had to imagine an invisible horse!

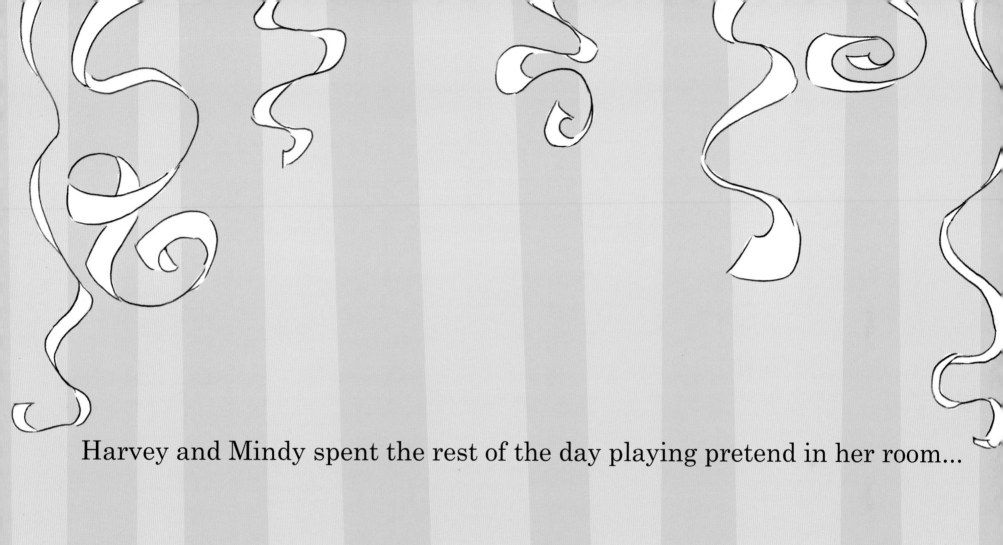

Harvey and Mindy spent the rest of the day playing pretend in her room...

They were jellyfish bobbling through the bluest blue sea.

They rode a purple elephant across a tightrope. . .

500 feet high!

They did the trapeze over the Grand Canyon with ease!

As the sun began its descent behind the horizon, Princess Mindy knew it was time for any child under the age of ten to go home, even a child mime.

Princess Mindy had never had so much fun...

and her piles of presents had remained untouched.

After calling off the search for an invisible horse,
Mindy arranged for her royal boat to take Harvey home.

Princess Mindy and her staff waved goodbye and shouted
thank you from the shore.

Her staff was most thankful of all.

Back in his own room, with his own things, Harvey thought to himself...

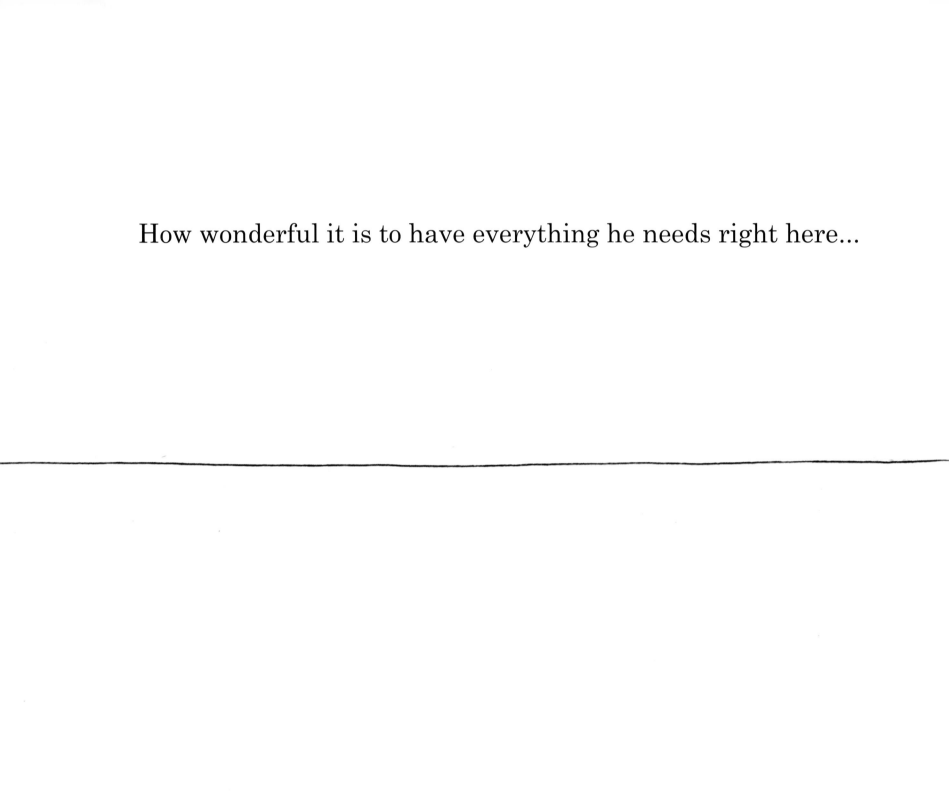

How wonderful it is to have everything he needs right here...

"Happiness is not something ready made. It comes from your own actions."

-Dalai Lama